Wenceslas

For Rory O'Kane
G.M.

For John and Myra
C.B.

WENCESLAS
A DOUBLEDAY BOOK 0 385 60535 8

Published in Great Britain by Doubleday,
an imprint of Random House Children's Books

This edition published 2005

1 3 5 7 9 10 8 6 4 2

Text copyright © Geraldine McCaughrean, 2005
Illustrations copyright © Christian Birmingham, 2005
Designed by Ian Butterworth

Set in Horley Old Style

RANDOM HOUSE CHILDREN'S BOOKS
61–63 Uxbridge Road, London W5 5SA
A division of The Random House Group Ltd

RANDOM HOUSE AUSTRALIA (PTY) LTD
20 Alfred Street, Milsons Point, Sydney,
New South Wales 2061, Australia

RANDOM HOUSE NEW ZEALAND LTD
18 Poland Road, Glenfield, Auckland 10, New Zealand

RANDOM HOUSE (PTY) LTD
Endulini, 5A Jubilee Road, Parktown 2193, South Africa

THE RANDOM HOUSE GROUP Limited Reg. No. 954009
www.kidsatrandomhouse.co.uk

A CIP catalogue record for this book is available from the British Library.

Printed and bound in Singapore

WENCESLAS

Geraldine McCaughrean

Illustrated by
Christian Birmingham

DOUBLEDAY

Snow laid siege to the city.

Winter, grim and grey, held the whole world in its grip.

Only one thing to do: draw the curtains and lock all the doors.

So great fires were burning in every palace grate, and twelve days of Christmas feasting lay ahead, silly with song and dance!

Even the tables, tottering under piles of food, seemed to want to dance with the big-bellied barrels of beer.

There would be minstrels and acrobats, actors, jesters, pipers and magic. Oh, and storytellers, of course. Peter always liked the storytelling best.

Then the King had to change everything. He did. He drew back a curtain, let in the draught and *looked out of the window*.

"Peter," he said.

"Yes, master?"

"Come here and tell me what you see."

Fields full of snow; the river frozen to a standstill; a deer scraping with one hoof, in hope of finding grass. Was it a game?

"Your kingdom, master?"

"And over there, among the trees? That young man?"

Peter had not noticed before the ragged, creeping figure; the bundle of firewood on the bent back looked like a hedgehog's spines.

"A peasant, master, yes."

"Do you know him?"

Know him? Peter, *know* him? A page at the royal palace of the King of Bohemia know a penniless peasant from the other end of the valley?

"I think he lives on the edge of the forest, master – near Saint Agnes' spring."

The King let the curtain fall back into place. "Then let's go and share Christmas with him!"

Peter could not make anyone believe him.

"You're going where?" said the Saddler, lifting the old sled down from its hook in the barn.

"You're going where?" said the Cook as Peter raided her pantry.

"You're going where?" said the Woodsman as Peter upset his woodpile.

"You're going *where*?" cried the guests as the two stripped a table of custards and tarts, knives and butter, puddings and fruit and candles.

"Out," said Peter, and even the wind outside howled with laughter.

Well, Peter could hardly believe it himself.

The cobbles in the yard were slippery as glass.

The moat was frozen gunmetal grey.

When Peter pushed open the postern gate, the storm broke in like a dog. It threw itself at their chests.

"It's all right for *him*," thought Peter. "*He* is big and strong and brave."

No horse could face such weather and live. And so they walked. The King and Peter bent their heads into the blizzard and walked.

"It's all right for *him*," thought Peter. "*He* is a king of the royal blood!"

There again, *he* was pulling the sled.

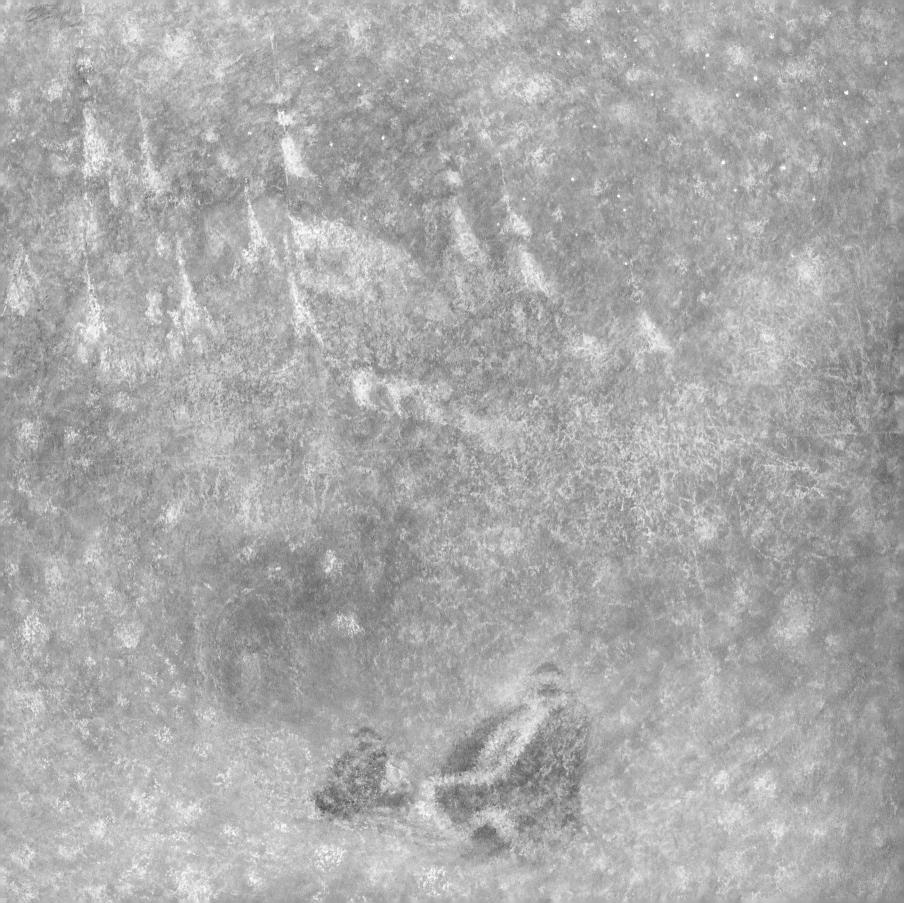

Snowflakes prick-prick-pricked at their faces. An east wind pick-pick-picked at their clothes. Stars like the points of nails hovered over their heads, sharp and ready to fall. They waded waist-deep in snow. Their breath froze in the air. Their lashes clogged with sleet. Their cloaks, dragging behind them, swept up swags of snow. And the blizzard closed in like an army of ghosts: *hoo woo!*

The night grew darker, the wind keener, and suddenly, quite suddenly, Peter's feet would not take another step.

He did not want to fail his master – he did not want to fall behind. But cold, like quicksand, was sucking him down – a numbing, stunning cold . . .

"Master! I don't . . . ! I'm sorry . . . ! I can't . . ."
Even the words froze in Peter's mouth.

The King turned and looked back.

"You can do it, Peter," he said, and smiled. "Do you see my footprints? Step where I stepped. You will be warmer that way. The cold won't bite so deep."

And so that is what Peter did. He followed in his master's footsteps. The holes left were big, like boots, and Peter slipped his feet into them. In went his feet and down, down into the warmth of a king's tracks.

And suddenly, somehow, Peter was not bogged down.

He was wearing the snow for boots!

Seven-league boots. Boots as big as a kingdom!

In boots like that, a boy can stride about like a king: *stamp! stamp! stamp!*

The blizzard now seemed less like looming ghosts than giant guiding angels, feather-cloaked in flakes of flying snow.

"Let's sing!" called Wenceslas above the bellowing of the wind.

And so they sang.

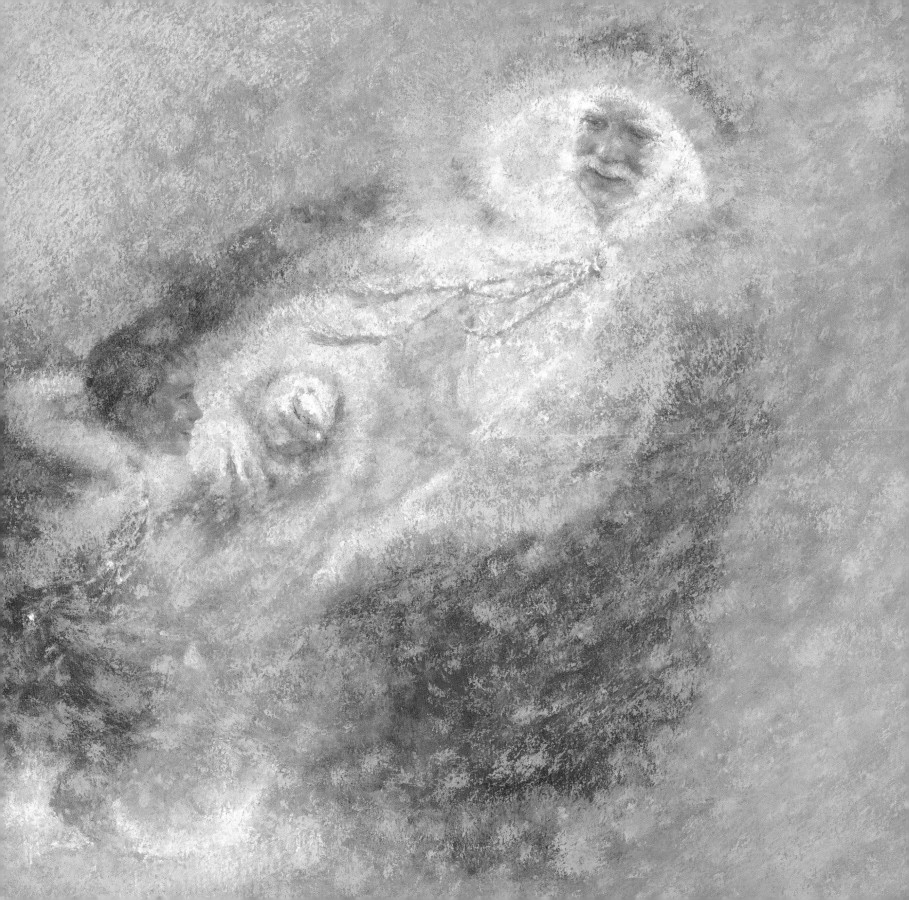

Even so, the forest is a fearful place full of dangers and dark.

Wasn't that a wolf howling, as well as the wind?

Wasn't that a bear staring at them, glaring at them, daring them to go one step farther . . . ?

Was the moon pulling a face – wincing at what lay in store . . . ?

Perhaps the bears, too, trod in those glowing prints. Perhaps the wolves warmed to their singing.

Or perhaps the wild beasts mistook Peter and the King for fellow beasts in the wild.

After all, who else would be out on such a night?

But all of a sudden there they were – safe and sound – at the end of nowhere, at the back of beyond.

"Peter, can it be you? Who is your friend?"

So in they went, Peter and the King –
lit the fire, hung the meat over the
flames, buttered the bread, sliced the
pies, broached the brandy and lit the
pudding. They peeled the cheese, they
cracked the nuts.

Peter even juggled some oranges.

Faces hollow with hunger watched
with open mouths.

The wind banged at the door.

Then suddenly, everyone smiled.

And after smiling, they laughed.

And after laughing, they sang –
the woodsman, his wife, the old folk,
Peter, the baby, the dog and the cat and
the King. They sang every last song they
knew and even a few they did not . . .

Although for some reason, Peter
could never remember afterwards how
the last song ended . . .

Next day, they fetched bright new tools from the sled –
hammer and plane and saw – and they helped fix up the
cottage: Peter and the King.

They patched the roof and mended the shutters, re-hung
the door and spread new rugs on the floor.

When it came time to leave, Peter laid his cloak over the
baby's cot, knowing he would not need it on the way home.

"Peter is following in my footsteps," the King explained.

It seemed a matter of moments, but there,

through the swirling blizzard and jagged trees, rose

the city crags all hung with snow.

What a sight they were, those ramparts, and

the palace beyond! Every window shone orange

with lights – like steps aglow up the sky.

There were faces too – at every window –

anxious, loving faces watching out for Wenceslas,

watching out for Peter.

All that was years ago, of course.

Now Peter sits by a Christmas fire, telling his story of Christmas kindness (because the King would never let him tell it, way back then).

Even when Peter's son draws back the curtain and lets in the driving snow, Peter only looks up and smiles.

"What do you see out there, Peterkin? Must we get out the sled again?"

Good King Wenceslas

Good King Wenceslas looked out,
    On the Feast of Stephen,
When the snow lay round about,
    Deep, and crisp, and even:
Brightly shone the moon that night,
    Though the frost was cruel,
When a poor man came in sight,
    Gathering winter fuel.

"Hither, page, and stand by me,
    If thou know'st it, telling,
Yonder peasant, who is he?
    Where and what his dwelling?"
"Sire, he lives a good league hence,
    Underneath the mountain,
Right against the forest fence,
    By St Agnes' fountain."

"Bring me flesh, and bring me wine,
    Bring me pine logs hither:
Thou and I will see him dine,
    When we bear them thither."
Page and monarch, forth they went,
    Forth they went together;
Through the rude wind's wild lament
    And the bitter weather.

"Sire, the night is darker now,
    And the wind blows stronger;
Fails my heart, I know not how;
    I can go no longer."
"Mark my footsteps, good my page;
    Tread thou in them boldly:
Thou shalt find the winter's rage
    Freeze thy blood less coldly."

In his master's step he trod,
    Where the snow lay dinted;
Heat was in the very sod
    Which the Saint had printed.
Therefore, Christian men, be sure,
    Wealth or rank possessing,
Ye who now will bless the poor,
    Shall yourselves find blessing.

J. M. Neale

THE STORY OF WENCESLAS

Duke Wenceslas of Bohemia was greatly loved by his people, though they knew nothing of any walk through the snow. He brought Christianity to his little corner of Germany; the grapes of his vineyard were crushed to make the Communion wine.

After his death, Wenceslas was declared a saint. Pilgrims streamed to his tomb in Prague and it is their footsteps through the German countryside that tell the true story of Wenceslas' goodness. The story of the snowy walk was written centuries later by an Englishman – J. M. Neale – a parable of kindness, bravery and charity suited to Christmastime and carols round the fire.